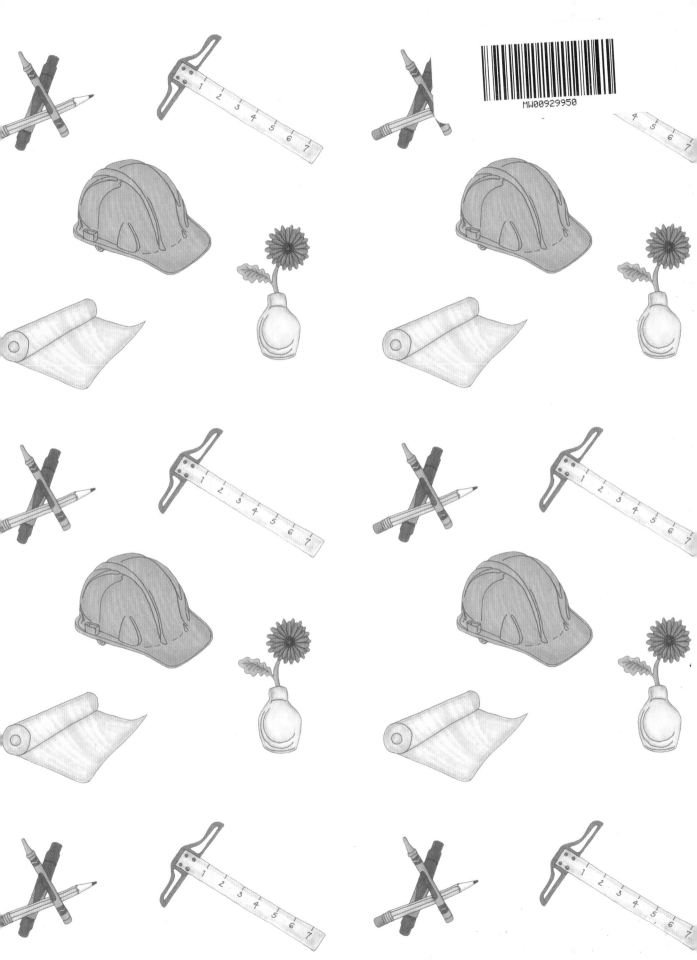

Special Dedication

Design Your World is dedicated to Cheryl Durst and Tracey Thomas. Cheryl showed us how design uplifts, unifies, and recognizes the very best of human beings. Cheryl and Tracey taught us that when a child discovers the power of design, it can be life-changing. Through their leadership in the International Interior Design Association, they are reshaping the profession of interior design to be more inclusive and accessible to all. We hope to do the same.

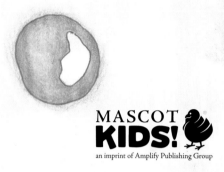

MASCOT KIDS!
an imprint of Amplify Publishing Group

www.mascotbooks.com

Design Your World

For more information, please contact:
Mascot Kids, an imprint of Amplify Publishing Group
620 Herndon Parkway, Suite 320
Herndon, VA 20170
info@mascotbooks.com

Library of Congress Control Number: 2022946331

CPSIA Code: PRKF1122A

ISBN-13: 978-1-63755-568-2

Printed in China

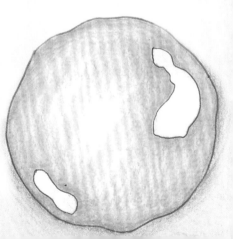

DESIGN YOUR WORLD

Maria VanDeman & Doug Shapiro
Illustrated by **Kenzie Leon Perry**

BEEP, BEEP, BEEP. The alarm went off, and Serena sat up in her bed. Her mom leaned on the doorway. "Good morning! I've set out your clothes. Get dressed and hurry out for breakfast."

Same as every morning, Serena wasn't quite ready to wake up, but she dragged herself out of bed. She wanted to wear her favorite new dress, but instead she put on her boring school clothes. Serena didn't get to choose what time to wake up . . . or what to eat for breakfast . . . or what to wear.

At school, Serena didn't even choose who she sat next to. She wanted to sit with her friends, but instead she was stuck next to Theo, who was always loud and silly.

Her teacher, Ms. Thomas, began the morning lesson. But instead of listening, Serena closed her eyes and imagined that she was the one making the rules.

Ms. Thomas paused by Serena's desk and leaned down to whisper, "Serena, since you have your eyes closed, why don't you tell me what you're dreaming about?"

Serena looked up slowly. "I just wish . . ." Serena paused. "I just wish I could decide things for myself, like where to sit and what to wear. I wish that I was in control."

"OK class," said Ms. Thomas. "Serena shared a valuable lesson with me. My challenge for all of you is to focus on what you can control, not what you cannot control. Your homework over the weekend is to write down things in your life that you can control."

Serena heard some of the students laughing, but it didn't bother her. In fact, nothing could bother Serena right now, because she knew after school she got to go to her favorite place . . . Grandma's house.

After school on the bus to Grandma's, Serena was thinking about what Ms. Thomas said, but she was having trouble coming up with things that she could control.

When she finally arrived, Serena raced up the porch steps past the two wooden rocking chairs and let out a deep, happy sigh. Grandma's house always felt *warm* and *safe*.

As Grandma opened the door for Serena, she saw the big, comfy sofa in the living room with a stack of coasters on the table. Walking into the cozy kitchen, she admired the shelf full of colorful cookbooks and smelled Grandma's freshly baked chocolate chip cookies.

Looking around, she noticed how neatly the pictures of her family lined up on the wall. The bright flowers and cheerful artwork made her feel at home, but she was still thinking about Ms. Thomas's question.

Serena slumped down at the kitchen table and watched her grandma as she began cooking dinner.

"Serena, what's wrong?" asked Grandma.

"Grandma," Serena said. "Ms. Thomas told me to focus on things I can control, but I can't think of anything."

"Hmm . . . Do you want to know my favorite thing to control?" said Grandma. "It's how I've designed and taken care of my home.

You know those rocking chairs on the porch? They were handmade by your great-grandfather, and I like to rock in them and watch the sunset. And do you know why the kitchen is right at the center of the home? The delicious smell of food brings everyone in the house together.

I chose an extra-wide sofa for the living room so all my grandkids can fit next to me. I wanted the family photos right near the door so my guests can see the people I care about most. The colorful walls and artwork remind me of how we always pick wildflowers together in the springtime. You see, Serena, everything has a place and a purpose."

As her grandma continued, Serena realized that her grandma's design was part of what gave her warm and happy feelings.

Serena began to imagine all the ways that she could design her own spaces. She wanted places like her home and school to feel even more special.

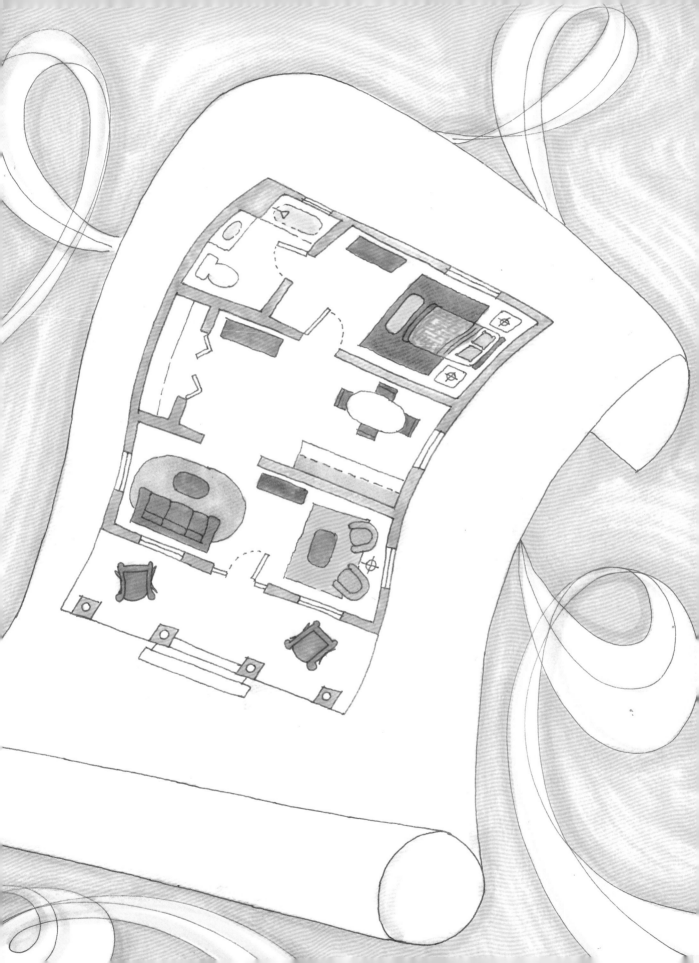

The next morning, Serena woke up excited to start on a plan for
her own room, a space where she was in control.

She made her bed and picked up her clothes. She cleaned her mirror and opened her window. She hung up colorful pictures from magazines. She rested pillows against the wall in the perfect spot for afternoon hangouts. Serena even went outside and found flowers to place in a jar on her dresser.

Serena designed a cheerful and cozy space for her and her friends, and it was even better than she had imagined. Over the weekend, she and her friends spent hours laughing and talking together.

It was the same room she'd always had, but now it gave her a brand-new feeling.

When Monday came and Serena went back to school, it didn't matter that she couldn't choose her breakfast or that she sat next to silly Theo. She had found the perfect answer to Ms. Thomas's question.

Ms. Thomas said, "Serena, since you started us down this journey, why don't you share with us what you can control?"

Serena dashed to the front of the class. "I can control the spaces around me. *I can design my world.*"

Ms. Thomas paused and looked around. "Wow. You're right, Serena. We all can! Why don't we try it right here and now. Any ideas?"

"Let's bring in some flowers!" shouted one student. "Let's move the bookshelf to make a reading corner!" said another. "Let's put our desks in a circle!" said Serena.

Before they knew it, the students had rearranged the whole classroom, opened the window blinds, cleaned their cubbies, organized the bookshelves, and hung their art.

The students cheered!

Ms. Thomas sat back in her chair and smiled. "How do you feel, class?" asked Ms. Thomas. "Much better!" said the class.

As Serena rode the bus home, she began to see all the ways to make the spaces around her better and, since then, she has never stopped.

Serena is all grown up now with kids of her own, and people all over the world call Serena and ask her to design a place just for them.

From schools and homes to restaurants and libraries, Serena continues to create spaces that feel **warm, happy, and safe,** just like her grandma's house.

Learn more about interior design and
create your own room design

ofs.com/design-your-world

Learn More

What is Interior Design?

"Interior design is how we experience space. It is a powerful, essential part of our daily lives and affects how we live, work, play, and even heal. Comfortable homes, functional workplaces, beautiful public spaces—that's interior design at work." - New York School of Interior Design

What do Interior Designers do?

Interior designers plan the layout of spaces within buildings—from where walls and doors are located, to paint colors, flooring, and furniture. They understand building codes, function of spaces, needs of their clients, and construction of the spaces they design. Interior designers not only create beautiful spaces but are also responsible for protecting the safety and well-being of the people using each space.

Where is Interior Design found?

All spaces within buildings are designed, including schools, restaurants, homes, offices, stores, hospitals, libraries, and community centers.

Who does Interior Design help?

You! Interior design affects the people within all the buildings and spaces we use daily. You, as a designer, have the power to influence your environment, community, and people's experiences and moods!

Giving Back

A portion of the proceeds from the sale of this book support the International Interior Design Association's Design Your World program. Design Your World is an education pipeline program driven by the mission to build equity and diversity in the design industry by providing high school students with exposure to the possibilities of a career in design. For more information about IIDA or Design Your World, visit www.IIDA.org.

About the Authors

Maria VanDeman, NCIDQ, LEED AP, Ind. IIDA

Maria VanDeman is a licensed interior designer, sales manager for OFS, and advocate for diversity, equity, and inclusion. Maria resides in Miami, Florida, with her husband, Nathan, and two children, Harper and Brooks.

Doug Shapiro, Ind. IIDA

Doug Shapiro is host of the podcast and media network Imagine a Place. Imagine a Place exists to help elevate the power of design and place in our life. He and his wife, Kim, have three children and live in the St. Louis area.

About the Illustrator

Kenzie Leon Perry, NCIDQ, IIDA

Kenzie Leon Perry is a licensed interior designer and creative director of Ze Haus Design Studio, a design firm specializing in creative interiors, fine art, bespoke home decor, and wallpaper. A native of Miami, Kenzie's designs are inspired by the Black and Caribbean diaspora and the tropics.

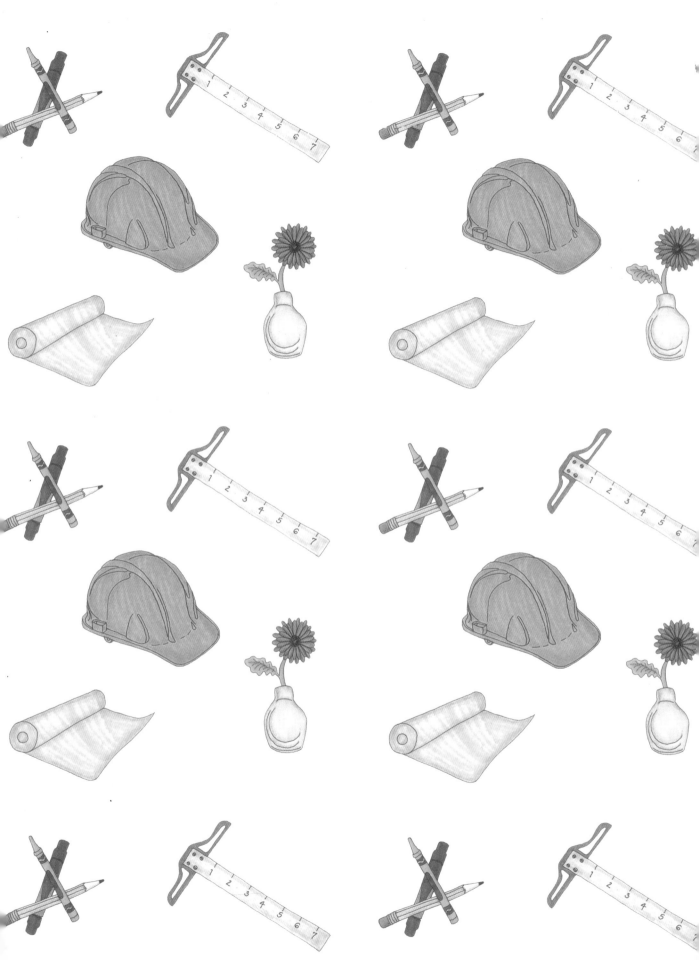